Rich Cat, Poor Cat

by
Bernard
Waber

for JAN GARY

ISBN 0-590-43091-2

12 11 10 9 8 7 6 5 4 3 2 1   9   9/8 0 1 2 3 4/9

Printed in the U.S.A.   23

SCHOLASTIC INC.

New York Toronto London Auckland Sydney

Some cats live in houses.

Scat is a street cat. Her home is anywhere she can stretch.

Some cats look out of picture windows,
smell rose petals, and go to sleep on downy pillows.

Scat's pillows are the coarse
cobblestones of the city streets.

Some cats have names like...

Ernestine

Abigail

Coco

Tasha

and even Cherie

Everyone knows Scat's name.
Whenever people see her coming,
they always say SCAT! SCAT!

7

Some cats are orange, tawny, or jet-black.

Scat is mousy gray.
(The kind of gray she likes best.)

Some cats go through life
surrounded by happy, friendly faces.

Scat looks everywhere for a friendly face.

Some cats have their own, very special towel . . .
their own, very special hairbrush . . .
their own, very special blanket . . .
their own, very special dish . . .
and their own very special chair.

There isn't anything very special in Scat's life.

Some cats have their portraits hung over the fireplace.

Scat would gladly pose.

Some cats like having their ears fondled and their backs gently stroked.

Scat would like this too.

Some cats have beauty care.
Their coats are brushed to a shimmering glow.

Scat does what she can to brighten up
her own somewhat matted coat.

Some cats travel in shiny black cars.

Scat travels on her own four feet.
(Mostly through alleys.)

Some cats have dinner served on a tray.
They are scolded if they refuse their broccoli.

Scat never refuses anything.

Some cats have to button up for nasty weather.
They wear green sweaters and matching green galoshes.

Just seeing them turns Scat green with envy.

Some cats must take a daily dose of vitamins
to give them extra energy and protect them from the virus.

There are days when Scat could do with a bit of extra energy.

Some cats, should they sneeze even once,
are put to bed and made to inhale deeply from the vaporizer.
They receive hundreds of get-well cards.

Scat never receives so much as a "bless you."

Some cats have "mustn'ts"...

mustn't eat the plants...

mustn't make faces at the canary...

mustn't claw the furniture...

mustn't climb the tables...

mustn't sleep in the linen closet...

mustn't cross the street...

and mustn't crawl into the bathtub.

Scat could use some "mustn'ts."

Some cats spend Sunday in the country.
They play hide-in-the-grass and climb tall trees.

Scat also climbs trees.
Often with precious few minutes to spare.

Some cats sail off for Europe.

Scat waves good-bye from the pier.

Some cats ride gondolas in Venice
and sunbathe on the Riviera.

It's hardly the Riviera for Scat, but at least it is the same sun.

Some cats are outrageously happy.

They have nothing more important on their minds than spending whole days chasing after their own tails.

Scat spends her days looking for food and her nights seeking shelter from driving winds and rain.

Most cats are somebody's cat.

Scat is nobody's cat.

A truck driver named Harry often says "Hi kitty," whenever he sees her.

Sometimes he even shares
his lunch with her.
But this isn't being
somebody's cat; not really.

One day, in the marketplace,
Scat met a little girl walking
with her mother.
The little girl smiled at Scat.
Scat smiled back.
"Poor little cat," said the girl.
"Poor little cat," said her mother.

They took Scat to their house.

Gave her dinner...

and a bed with a pillow...

and they named her Gwendolyn.